Allure

AMY LAURENS

OTHER WORKS

Find other works by the author at www.amylaurens.com

Allure

INKLET #55

AMY LAURENS

Inkprint PRESS

www.inkprintpress.com

Print ISBN: 978-1-925825-57-2
eBook ISBN: 9781393059028

www.inkprintpress.com

National Library of Australia Cataloguing-in-Publication Data
Laurens, Amy 1985 –
Allure
40 p.
ISBN: 978-1-925825-57-2
Inkprint Press, Canberra, Australia
1. Fiction—Romance—Science Fiction 2. Fiction—Short Stories

First Print Edition: April 2021
Cover design © Inkprint Press
Interior art © Amy Laurens

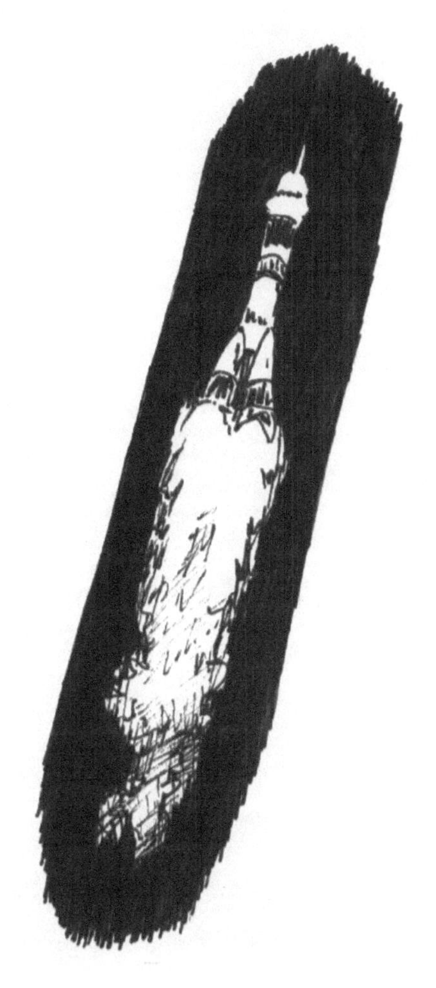

ALLURE

Sara gripped Ash's hand fiercely as the wind tangled her brown hair in her mouth. The summer night lay hot and humid, full of beaches even though the closest was at least a hundred kilometres away; a night full of pregnant pauses and insect humming, rocked intermittently by explosions of sound and light; a night when, despite the show, sensible people would be indoors in their air conditioning, watching the Christmas carols or yet another clichéd family holiday movie.

The launches were old news; ships had been departing continuously for the better part of a month, and Christmas was a greater novelty.

Sara swallowed and squeezed Ash's hand tighter. Not for her. Instead of the traditional family meal by candlelight, she stood on the hilltop with her ex-fiancé, fingers entwined, watching the rockets streak skywards. *Christmas is a stupid time to schedule launches,* she thought vehemently.

Christmas was for homecomings and returns, not departures to worlds unknown. But the Government called, and Ash was duty-bound to answer, and in less than twelve hours he'd be on board one of those streaks of light that rumbled like the very thunder of the gods, a meteoroid shooting up in reverse to join the stars in space.

"Are you okay?" Ash said.

He meant it to be quiet, a question full of warmth and concern, but over the ships and the wind he had to shout close to her ear.

Sara nodded, rescuing more hair from between her lips and tucking it futilely around her ear. "I'm fine."

She had to be, didn't she? She was not the only fiancée scheduled to be abandoned on Christmas Day. Each fiery streak in the sky represented at least a score of soldiers, plus a host of supporting crew and technicians, all headed to Tarne, where heroes were in great demand.

Abruptly, Sara kicked the railing that enclosed the lookout. Let Tarne fight their own war.

What help would a thousand extra soldiers be, let alone the single one who was supposed to be hers?

The Alphs out-numbered humanity ten to one, and the government could empty the entire planet to Tarne to aid in the war effort and it wouldn't faze the invaders in the slightest.

Ash gathered her in his arms, word-
less as another launch shattered Sara's
composure just a little more. She pressed her face against his shoulder and
swallowed hard to ease the ache in her
throat, her chest, her eyes. She would
not cry, she wouldn't. This was his last
night on Earth likely for the rest of his
life and, dammit, it would be a good
one.

"Let's go," she said against his ear.

"Where?" he said loudly, smooth-
ing her hair from both their faces.

"Anywhere. Away. I don't want to
watch them anymore."

He nodded and took her hand,
squeezing it as he led her to their car.

On the other side of town, the rocket launches still shook the world like
bombs, but as Sara climbed out of the
air-con of the car and felt her shirt

plaster against her skin in the humidity, she didn't care. They'd pulled up at the Hotel Grande, the only hotel in town but grand enough for all of that.

Sara plucked at her shirt, but gave it up for a bad job when she realised how soaked it was. The wind on the hilltop had masked some of the humidity, but here in the low-lying suburbs, the air was still and heavy. And anyway, she thought, glancing down again, at least it gave the illusion of cleavage.

Ash wrapped his arm around her shoulders. "Come on," he muttered.

Sara's stomach quickened with adrenalin as she eyed the sparkling stars and wondered what she would do when her entire future was swept away to one of them. She shrugged to clear her head, and they entered the hotel.

"One night," Ash said curtly at the desk, handing over their id cards.

The desk clerk looked at them knowingly as he picked up Ash's military ID, sympathy warming his hazel eyes. "Room 106," he said, handing them the door card. "On the house. Lifts are over there."

Clutching Ash's hand like he might change his mind, Sara strode towards the lifts and swiped the card. The doors shushed open and she hurried in, closing her eyes and listening as the doors shut and the lift whirred into motion. Nothing. No rockets to break the drone of electric and mechanical noises, no wind to buffet her self-control.

Ash slipped his arms around her waist from behind and nuzzled against her ear. "Quiet in here."

Sara smiled tautly. "Perfect then." She twisted around to face him, wrapped her arms around his neck, and kissed him exactly like this was his last night on Earth.

The lift dinged and opened, and over Ash's shoulder Sara caught a glimpse of an almost-elderly lady with her mouth set in a disapproving line. Ash noticed and flushed red, but Sara tucked her arm in his and gave the woman a smile that could crack diamonds. "Military," she said.

She didn't wait to see if the woman's expression softened. Pity could be a sledgehammer sometimes.

Their room was only a few doors down, and as she clicked the card into the door and turned the handle, Ash leaned warm against her. "I like you like this," he murmured.

"Like what?" Sara said stiffly, drawing him into the room.

He smirked at her, eyes sparkling. "Decisive."

"Good," she said, pressing him against the wall. "Then you won't complain if I do this."

An hour or so later, Sara wrapped herself in the hotel's white bath robe, turning up the collar and rubbing the stiff fabric against her cheeks. If she closed her eyes and imagined really hard, it almost felt like Ash's stubble. She'd have to remember that.

She glanced at him, sprawled out on the bed in nothing but his coffee skin, eyes closed, chest rising and falling softly. It was almost impossible to imagine him as a soldier when she saw him like this. With the light just right, he might have been nothing more than a boy—a child playing at grownups, playing at being a soldier.

She twirled the ring on her left hand and bit the inside of her lip. Goosebumps rose on her arms; she rubbed at them, annoyed. Why did hotels always overcompensate with the air conditioning? Didn't they realise that half the hotel population was likely to be clothe-less at any given time?

The blinds tapped at the window in a sudden breeze and Sara crossed to them. She raised them all the way up and flung the window wide, welcoming the fresh, warm air. It still smelled like the beach, all hot stone and salt, and Sara thought of all the plans Ash and she had made for their perfect beach wedding.

Her lips tightened and her eyes pricked. Scrunching up her face, Sara redirected her gaze skyward. Brilliant points of light; a net full of ockle-shells as deep in their ocean as planets far away; glow worms, luring in their prey.

Yes, that was it: alluring little pretties designed to tempt humanity away from where it belonged. If man had never gone to the stars, none of this would be happening—the war, the evacuations, her cancelled wedding.

"Let's get married," she said suddenly.

Ash shifted in the sheets. "What?"

"Tonight. Before you go. There has to be someplace open that can do it." She paced the windows, tugging on the belt of the robe.

Ash propped himself on an elbow and eyed her thoughtfully. "You really want to come?"

Sara stopped, mouth open. "Oh." She'd forgotten about that, the newest instalment in a long line of ridiculous government regulations: the population of Tarne was being decimated; nurses were in short supply, but so too were mothers, and in what was set to be a decades-long war of attrition, the team with the highest birth-rate was the likely victor.

The Alphs had started with the obvious advantage—far superior numbers—but humans held a trump card: a reproduction cycle fifty times shorter than that of the Alph females. If the colony could just hold on in the meantime, twenty or thirty years might be long enough to reverse the numbers.

Visions of her planned life flashed through Sara's head: her wedding on the beach; a house in the Adelaide hills with a picket fence and two Cocker Spaniels; a baby's nursery, decorated in pastel shades of blue, and pink, and yellow; her mother, hair greyed—though skin strangely unwrinkled in Sara's imaginings—and holding a tiny grandbaby; a studio out the back of the house where Sara made her world-famous art.

The beach wedding was gone, that much was certain. Even if she found another man to love, she could never marry him on a beach, not now, not after Ash. The rest she still might have, if she was lucky—and if the war did not steal another husband from her. But really, was it worth it?

She crossed the room and sat down next to Ash. He didn't reach for her, watching her carefully instead, wary, like a roo deciding whether or not to flee. Sara searched his face, tracing with her eyes the curve of his cheek, the straight, proper line of his nose, the clear, high forehead, and finally alighting on his golden-brown eyes. If she married him, if she went with him —well, she might still have the house and the studio and the dogs. (They had dogs on Tarne, didn't they?)

The babies were a foregone conclusion, at least, if she did decide to go.

"Do you want me to?" she said at last.

Ash stiffened upright, gaze so intense Sara had to look away. "Of course I do," he said quietly. "You know I do."

She shrugged. "You never asked me to." Cancelling the wedding had seemed like the obvious solution when Ash had received his orders, and as no one had ever suggested otherwise, Sara'd never let herself consider anything else. Her life was here, after all.

But then, so had his been.

Ash took up her hand, holding it like a bird between cupped fingers. "I could never ask that of anyone I loved," he said, and his voice was low and fervent and sent shivers up her spine. "You've seen the pictures. You know what it will be like."

She had, and she did; there would be no white picket fence, and the studio would probably be more of a shack. But the question now was, did that matter?

Her gaze fluttered up to his again, and she inhaled sharply. "I won't force myself on you," she said. "I do know what it will be like, and you'll have enough to deal with without a brand-new, totally naïve girl-wife in tow. Though it can't be *much* worse than Woomera," she said, grinning weakly.

Ash didn't react, and she swallowed, throat suddenly dry. "Ask me," she whispered as her pulse raced. "Ask me, and I'll go."

"I love you, Sara," Ash said, reaching out to run his thumb over her cheek. "Don't leave me."

"You're the one who's leaving," she whispered, pressing her eyes closed.

"Come with me." His breath was warm and humid on her cheek and adrenalin and longing surged through her.

"Yes," she breathed.

He kissed her, long and slow, exactly like they had the rest of their lives to spend together, and as they felt back against the sheets, limbs and lives entangled, another rocket rumbled skyward, sparkling in the sky.

THE MAKING OF
ALLURE

I wrote this story for the SFR Brigade's inaugural anthology, *Tales From The SFR Brigade*. That was back in 2013, right around the time I was getting back into writing again after having my son.

I'd never written anything science-fictiony before, despite enjoying reading and watching the genre. And I'd certainly never written sfr, or science-fiction romance, before.

I'm not even sure I'd *read* much science-fiction romance, at least outside of Liana Brooks' work, which I was reading as a beta reader before publication.

And, while we're confessing things here... I'm not even sure I was a member of the SFR Brigade at the time of writing this, and having it accepted! I did have plenty of friends in it, however, and obviously they were happy enough to have me. Lovely that it all worked out; let's imagine it did so for Sara and Ash as well.

(In fact, we don't need to imagine this: one day, I might get around to writing the novel I have plotted that finishes their storyline, and they do, indeed, get a hard-fought-for Happily Ever After.)

Read more by Amy Laurens!

TRUST ISSUES

WARM STEAM FILLED THE AIR AROUND Becca, faintly scented with fake apples from her shampoo. The hot water pattered down on her back, turning her skin red and, in theory, soothing away her tension. Of course, that would have been more easily facilitated had she not been in the midst of performing the contortions necessary to get her legs shaved, but she'd feel better once she was done. Probably.

Up, rinse, up, rinse; she scraped the blossom-pink razor over her pale legs, shaking it out in the main stream of the shower water at the top of each stroke. Steam billowed up in her face as she curled over her leg, warm against her cheeks and the inside of her nose.

There. Nearly done.

Honestly, the whole thing was an exercise in pointless futility. It wasn't like the wolf was going to be staring at her legs. And if he did, so what? Why did she care what he thought?

She didn't, that's what. Jaw clenching, Becca pressed shower water from her eye with the tips of her fingers.

One last stroke.

Becca inhaled sharply as the razor sliced the sensitive skin over her Achilles heel, removing a good slice of flesh and making the water run momentarily red.

She grabbed at her ankle with her free hand, trying to stem the bleeding with her thumb, and nearly slipped on the wet tiles. Her elbow smacked the bottles of hair products that lined the shower's shelf—and the shelf itself— and she hopped madly, trying to regain her balance. Her weight fell against the cold glass of the shower screen—and the door screaked open, dumping her unceremoniously on the mat.

"Ow." That was going to bruise her butt.

Disgusted, Becca threw the razor back into the shower and scrambled to her feet. She reached in and turned the water off, realising as she did that her right elbow was about as tender as her butt would be in the morning. She flung her dark blonde, wet hair out of her eyes. So much for getting pretty.

Stupid date.

Stupid wolf.

Red streaks on the mat caught her eye as she snagged her white towel off the rail: her heel, still dripping blood.

Bloody hell.

Literally.

She gathered her wet hair to one side, picking it off her shoulders and neck, wrapped the towel around herself, and hobbled to the vanity. Somewhere in there, lost amid cobwebbed piles of lotions, powders and unused potions, was a packet of bandaids.

Becca crouched awkwardly, stretching into the back of the cupboard that stank of bleach and toothpaste—and jumped as her sore elbow connected with something cold: a festering bottle of nail polish that was only too happy to jump off the shelf and smash on the floor, bleeding its awful browny-coral innards all over the second bath mat.

The chemical scent of the polish hit her nostrils. *Urgh. Someone remind me why I am doing this?*

Perching on the edge of the bath, Becca applied the bandaid, a giant strip wider than two of her fingers, its 'flesh' tones doing nothing to blend in with the complexion her grandmother had liked to call porcelain. "Bloody Irish," she muttered.

She smoothed the plaster down, snatched up the bloodied bathmat and took it to the laundry, then stalked back to her room to dress.

Underwear, now that was a question. Not that there was any *question* of him *seeing* her underwear. She was widowed, not desperate. Even if, just occasionally, when he turned his big stupid wolf eyes on her she lost her mind just a little bit remembering what sex had been like.

But back to the underwear, she reminded herself as she finished towelling off and used the damp towel to twist up her hair. She didn't trust him as far as she could throw him, which given she doubted she could even lift him off the ground amounted practically to not at all—but could she really bring herself to go plain black cotton on a date?

Ah, screw it. It wasn't like the dress was that fitted or anything. Comfy it was. Becca fished her favourite pair of black undies out from the crumpled mess in her top drawer, donned a sensible—if slightly uplifting—bra, and from the very back of her other top drawer snatched out an old, dusty satin pencil case, the magenta one with the floral embroidery.

Despite nearly stabbing herself in the eye with mascara she hadn't applied in years, and overdoing it with the big round hairbrush and the hairdryer so it looked like she was wearing a 1960s wig for a few minutes until she managed to de-volumise things a bit, Becca managed to finish getting ready with a relative minimum of fuss.

She slipped into her little black dress—always go with a classic on the first date, she'd decided; she still wasn't actually sure whether she wanted to impress the wolf or scare him away—slipped her phone, driver's licence and bank card into the cunningly placed pocket, straightened the short sleeves, and squished into a pair of heels that were dangerously tall and stunningly gorgeous: black satin with red and gold oriental designs brocaded into the fabric, nearly six inches high.

She wobbled for the first few steps before remembering how to balance right in them: Weight on the toes, pretend the shoes aren't really there, just tip-toe along with your calves tight and your core strong.

You got this.

She caught sight of her reflection in her dresser mirror and sighed, confidence deflating. It had been so long since she'd done this. She'd been married to that two-faced jerk Nick for nearly three years, but they'd dated for another four or five before that.

She hadn't first-dated since she was what, eighteen? Nineteen?

Becca ran a hand over her forehead and exhaled. Nick was gone now. He might have stolen eight years of her life and literally any chance she ever had at having children of her own—the familiar flutter of regret and longing trembled through her stomach—but he was gone.

And the wolf was safe, at least inasmuch as he wouldn't lie to her upfront like Nick had.

Probably.

Maybe.

She hoped.

Really, there was no way to know. And trust wasn't exactly her specialty, when she was used to being able to detect lies and secrets right there in the head of anybody around her.

Urgh. Why, why am I doing this? This is such a bad idea.

As if on cue, her phone buzzed.

A message from her sister Clare: *I know he's picking you up in fifteen minutes, which means you're moping around wondering why you let me bully you into this, so I'm reminding you of our little bargain.*

Besides. He's gorgeous. It'll be good for you.

Becca's lips quirked to a half smile. Her sister knew her all too well—hence the bargain, whereby Becca would be subjected to an endless stream of potential suitors every time she visited Clare if she didn't agree to a date with the wolf. And simply avoiding Clare's house wouldn't have worked; Clare would have just hauled the suitors to her.

A knock sounded at the door.

Adrenalin leapt through Becca's stomach and she bolted upright, stuffing her phone back into her pocket, then heading to the door.

"I'm sorry," Wolf-boy said as she opened it. "I know it's not fashionable to be early, but the traffic was better than I'd planned."

He'd left his longish hair down, a perfectly-styled tangle of honey-brown waves that screamed to be touched, and although he was wearing a dark suit, he'd left his baby-blue shirt open at the neck, and the combination did little to hide the sheer breadth and power of his shoulders.

His golden eyes drilled through her, soft and amused and completely, utterly focused on her.

Becca realised she was staring and closed her mouth, working the inside of her lower lip between her teeth.

So the wolf scrubbed up well. That changed nothing. She'd known since she'd met him that he was sex-on-legs. That, she'd learned the hard way, was not even *close* to the top ten most important things in a relationship. "It's okay," she said. "I'm ready."

She stepped out the door, forcing him to step aside for her, and locked up the house. "Ready?" The smile she gave him was too bright, brittle like it might crack any moment, and she tried to relax.

He studied her carefully for just an instant too long, but nodded. "Sure, let's go."

Keep reading! Head to
www.inkprintpress.com/amylaurens/
secretbreaker/trustissues/
to buy your copy now!

Amy Laurens is an Australian author of fantasy fiction for all ages. Although she never had to make the decision to move literal planets for her beloved, her beloved did move interstate so they could get married. Who says stories don't come true?

Amy has also written the award-winning portal-fantasy *Sanctuary* series about Edge, a 13-year-old girl forced to move to a small country town because of witness protection (the first book is *Where Shadows Rise*), the humorous fantasy *Kaditeos* series, following newly graduated Evil Overlord Mercury as she attempts to acquire a castle, the young adult series *Storm Foxes*, about love and magic and family in small town Australia, and a whole host of non-fiction.

INKLETS

Collect them all! Released on the 1ˢᵗ and 15ᵗʰ of each month.

INKLET #055
Allure
AMY LAURENS

INKLET #056
The LIES We KNOW
LIANA BROOKS

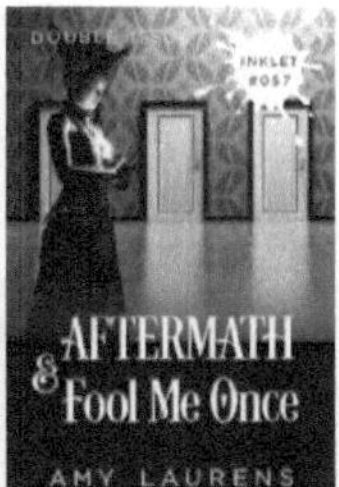
DOUBLE
INKLET #057
AFTERMATH
& Fool Me Once
AMY LAURENS

INKLET #058
Purity
An Age Of Uniforms Story
AMY LAURENS

INKLET #059
Saved
AMY LAURENS

INKLET #060
A Kiss is the Secret
AMY LAURENS

INKLET #061
A Changing Tides Story
Fire Bright
AMY LAURENS

INKLET #062
Hades AND Persephone
LIANA BROOKS

INKLET #063
Just So Long As You're Happy
AMY LAURENS

INKLET #064
Theft Of A Lifetime
LIANA BROOKS

INKLET #065
Shoe
AMY LAURENS

INKLET #066
Published AUTHOR
LIANA BROOKS

DOUBLE ISSUE
INKLET #067
THE REMARKABLE INSIGHT OF JELLYBEANS, & Understanding
AMY LAURENS

INKLET #068
Desperate Measures
AMY LAURENS

INKLET #069
Rock-a-bye
LIANA BROOKS

INKLET #070
the Other Carly
AMY LAURENS

INKLET #071
Bs By Bioluminescent Light
AMY LAURENS

INKLET #072
Even Villains Grant Wishes
A Heroes & Villains Story
LIANA BROOKS